For Elizabeth and Amy Dale,
with love and fond memories of our Canadian
adventures searching for scary bears!
And for Louise Bolongaro,
with many thanks for her wonderful
vision and guidance.
E.D.

For my real-life Daddy Bear – John Nigel.
P.M.

First published in 2016 by Nosy Crow Ltd
The Crow's Nest, 10a Lant Street
London SE1 1QR
www.nosycrow.com

ISBN 978 0 85763 646 1 (HB)
ISBN 978 0 85763 647 8 (PB)

Nosy Crow and associated logos are trademarks and/or registered
trademarks of Nosy Crow Ltd.

Text copyright © Elizabeth Dale 2016
Illustrations copyright © Paula Metcalf 2016

The right of Elizabeth Dale to be identified as the author and
of Paula Metcalf to be identified as the illustrator of this work has been asserted.

A CIP catalogue record for this book is available from the British Library.

Printed in Turkey by Imago.
Papers used by Nosy Crow are made from wood grown in sustainable forests.

1 3 5 7 9 10 8 6 4 2 (HB)
1 3 5 7 9 10 8 6 4 2 (PB)

Nothing Can Frighten a Bear

Elizabeth Dale illustrated by Paula Metcalf

nosy crow

Deep, deep in the woods, with the moon shining bright,
Some bears snuggled up in their beds for the night.

There was Mummy Bear, Daddy Bear . . .

Grace and then Ben . . .

And Baby Bear, too,
who lay dreaming,
but then . . .

As Baby Bear wriggled
and stretched out a paw,
He **suddenly** woke
when he heard a loud . . .

. . . roar!

"**Help!**" Baby cried. "There's a monster about!
He's coming to get me – I just heard him shout."
"Don't worry," said Mummy Bear, stroking his head.
"There **aren't** any monsters. Let's go back to bed."

But Baby Bear sniffled, "How can you be **sure?**
I **can't** sleep until I know **what** made that roar!"

"In that case," said Daddy Bear, grabbing a light,

"Why don't we go looking for monsters **tonight?**

You'll see that there's nothing so scary out there.
And anyway, **nothing** can frighten a **bear!**"

So **five** bears went marching out through the tall trees,
When Mum heard a noise and cried,
"Everyone – **freeze!**"

So all the bears stopped – could a **monster** be near?
But out of the darkness there trotted a . . . **deer!**

"You see," Daddy laughed, "there's no monster out there.
And anyway, **nothing** can frighten a **bear.**"

The little bears said, "We're as **brave** as can be!"
But no one saw Mummy get caught in a . . .

. . . tree!

So **four** bears went striding out into the night,
When Ben saw a splash and squealed, "There! On our right!"
They stopped where they stood on a slippery log,
Then out of the water there hopped a big . . . **frog!**

"You see," Daddy laughed, "there's no monster out there.
And anyway, **nothing** can frighten a **bear**."

"Keep going," said Daddy. "There's no need to scream."
But no one saw Ben slip and fall in the . . .

. . . stream!

So **three** bears squelched on down a thick, muddy track,

When Grace said, "What's that? Something brushed past my back!"

"Perhaps it's a monster," thought Baby. "Oh no!"

But out of the darkness there swooped a black . . . **crow!**

"You see," Daddy laughed, "there's no monster out there.
And anyway, **nothing** can frighten a **bear.**"

They sploshed and they splashed as they tramped through the muck,
But nobody noticed that Grace had got . . .

. . . stuck!

Now **two** bears were sleepily wandering on.
They **still** hadn't noticed the others had gone.
The lamp gave a flicker and started to fade.
"I want to go home," Baby said.
"I'm **afraid.**"

"All right then," said Daddy, "let's get you to bed.
There aren't any monsters. It's just as I said!
I told you that **nothing** can frighten a **bear.**"
But then he looked round and saw . . .

. . . nobody there!

"But **where** have the others gone?" Daddy Bear cried.
"I thought they were here, walking right by our side!
Perhaps they decided to go home to bed,
Or . . . maybe a **monster** has got them instead!"

Then out of the darkness a **shadow** appeared.
"Oh no!" Daddy cried. "This is worse than I feared!
Quick, take my paw, Baby, and hide behind me.
There isn't just **one** monster here, there are . . .

. . . three!

Just look! They're so **fierce.**
How their scary eyes stare.
Now **that** is a sight that can frighten a **bear.**"

"Oh, Baby," he shuddered,
"we **must** run away!"
But just then the scariest monster roared . . .

Poor Daddy Bear shivered
while sucking his thumb,
But Baby Bear giggled and said,
"That's my **mum!**"

"You **sillies,**" said Mummy Bear. "Surely you see?
We may look a mess, but it's Ben, Grace and me."
"It's you!" Daddy cried. "Oh, how silly I feel.
I thought for a second that monsters were **real.**"

So **five** bears went home, feeling ready for bed.

"We'll **all** stick together this time," Daddy said.

Deep, deep in the woods, with the moon shining bright,

The bears snuggled up in their beds for the night.

When **suddenly** everyone looked all around,
For **something** had just made a strange . . .

. . . growly sound!

"I'm **sure** there's a monster now!" Baby Bear cried.

"No, Baby, it's **you!**" all the others replied.

"It wasn't a monster that scared you before.

You woke yourself up with your **own roary** . . .

. . . snore!"